THIS BOOK BELONGS TO

· ·

To my beautiful and silly girl, Ellianna Jaymes.

You're going to be the best big sister one day.

I also dedicate this story to my amazing husband, Brandon,

adventurous sister, Jessica,

and my very supportive parents.

Text copyright © 2018 by Lindsay B. Achtman

Illustrations copyright © 2018 by Andra Morosan

Edited by: Erika Westrich, Sam Cabbage, and Calico Editing and Author Services

For The Love Of Literacy LLC 1760 S Telegraph Rd #300, Bloomfield Hills, MI 48302

First Edition, 2019. Printed in China.

Identifiers: ISBN: 978-1-7335250-0-8

Library of Congress Control Number: 2019900373

@achtman.author

I HOPE IT'S A PUPPY!

WRITTEN BY LINDSAY ACHTMAN · ILLUSTRATED BY ANDRA MOROSAN

For The Love Of Literacy, LLC

Mommy's having a baby,
and says it's quite a blessing!
I hear it's a surprise,
but I'm super great at guessing!

I touch my Mommy's belly.
It feels so soft and fluffy.
"Oh, Mommy! Mommy!" I declare,
"It must be a...

...PLAYFUL PUPPY!"

5

Courageous is my puppy,
performing amazing tricks!
Jumping through high hoops,
and catching gigantic sticks!

But wait...It can't be a puppy,
Mommy's belly has a horn!
"Oh, Mommy! Mommy!" I sing with joy,
"It must be a...

We will strut into school,
leaving glitter in our path.
Friends giggle and teachers glare,
as my unicorn does math!

10

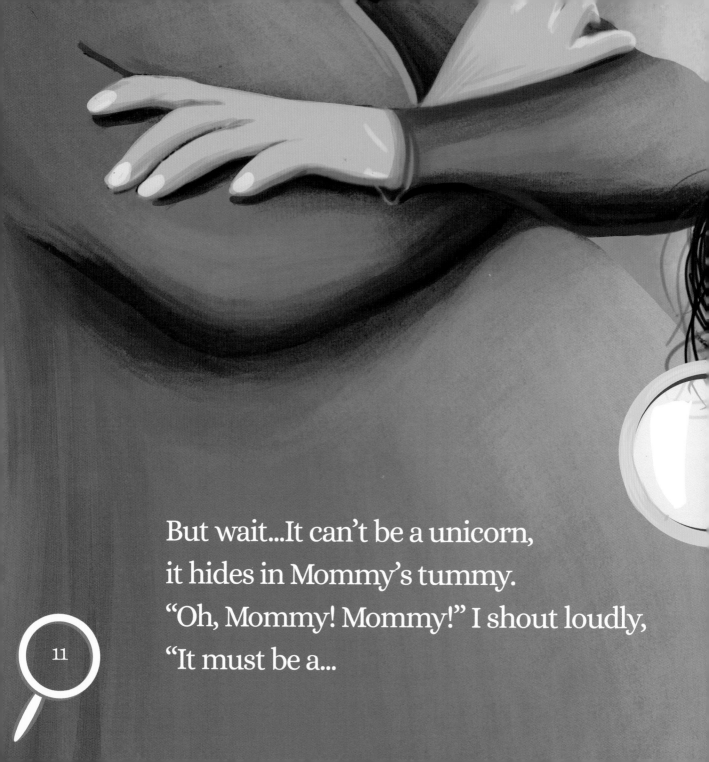

But wait...It can't be a unicorn,
it hides in Mommy's tummy.
"Oh, Mommy! Mommy!" I shout loudly,
"It must be a...

12

...BASHFUL BUNNY!"

My bunny and I will eat veggies,
like crunchy carrots and lettuce.
We will hop around the yard,
acting like a menace!

14

But wait...It can't be a bunny,
I hear a hoot and howl.
"Oh, Mommy! Mommy!" I whisper,
"It must be a...

...SNOWY OWL!"

17

On arched wings we will soar,
through each frosty mountain pass.
Mommy replies with giggles,
"That sound is only gas!"

18

But wait...It can't be an owl,
Mommy goes teeter totter.
"Oh, Mommy! Mommy!" I exclaim,
"It must be a...

...SEA OTTER!"

We will hold hands in the water,
then sunbathe on the sand.
Cracking a clam with a rock,
will make our meal grand!

But wait... It can't be an otter,
she says it will be like me.
"Oh, Mommy! Mommy!" I cry out,
"It must be a...

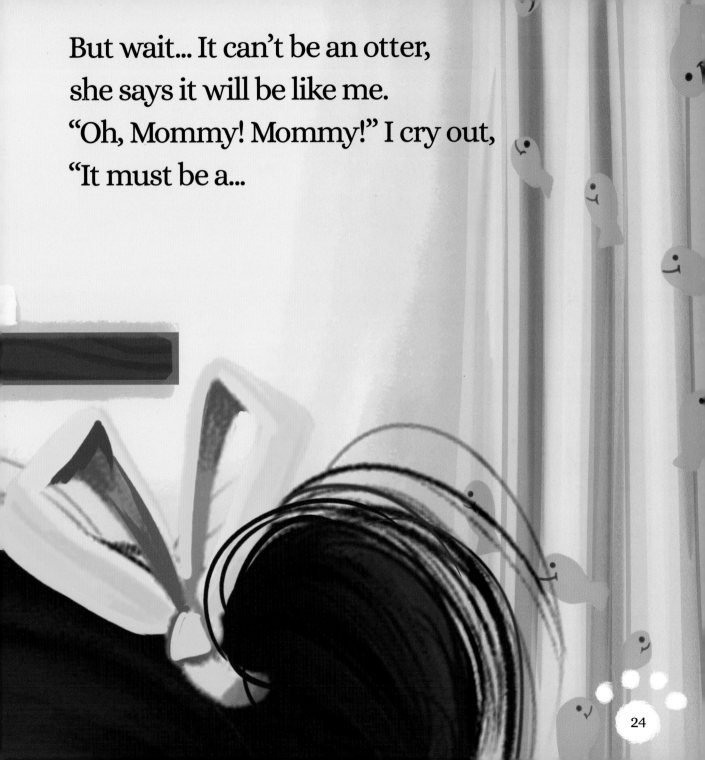

...MONKEY!"

25

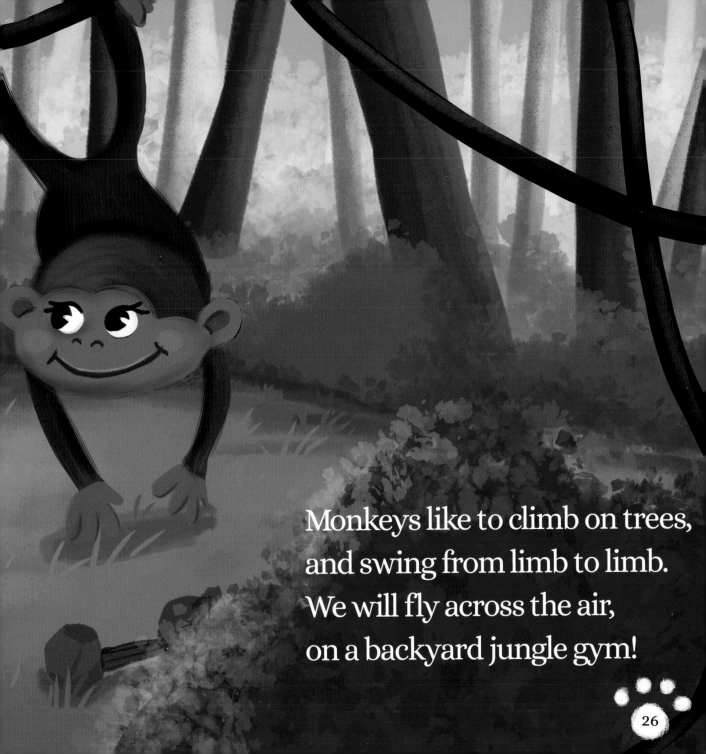

Monkeys like to climb on trees,
and swing from limb to limb.
We will fly across the air,
on a backyard jungle gym!

26

But wait... Mommy shows me an ultrasound and to my pleasant surprise...

"Oh, Mommy! Mommy! It's a small human, who will one day be full-size!"

I squeeze the photo tightly,
imagining all the fun we'll have together!
Having a sibling means having a best friend,
that'll stick with me forever!

We don't know if it's a boy or girl
so I'll continue pressing...
Luckily, as you all now know,

I AM SUPER GREAT AT GUESSING!

Meet the Author

Lindsay Achtman is a passionate teacher and loving mother who pours her personal experiences into her writing. Lindsay captures the perspective of a child perfectly in her stories, as she uses humor and poetry to teach lessons and ignite the imagination. She looks at life as an adventure waiting to be explored. When she is not writing or in the classroom, Lindsay enjoys spending time with her family and puppy, Lola, playing games, having picnics in the park, swimming in the lake, and cheering on her favorite Michigan sports teams. Lindsay Achtman is also the proud author of the story, "The Day The Swing Stopped."

Meet the Illustrator

Andra is a child wandering through the magic land of colors, with a MA and BA in her pocket and a paintbrush in her hand. Inspired by the amazing little girls at her art course, she discovered that she loves drawing for kids.

Andra loves to be surrounded by magical characters as she gets to know the story of every hero and meets storytellers from all around the world.